MARK WEST

POLLY

STORMBLADE PRODUCTIONS

STORMBLADE PRODUCTIONS

Published 2016 by Stormblade Productions

ISBN: 978-0-9935336-1-7

Copyright © Mark West 2016

STORMBLADE PRODUCTIONS

POLLY

STORMBLADE PRODUCTIONS

For

Alison & Matthew, as always

STORMBLADE PRODUCTIONS

Acknowledgements

Thanks to Mum & Dad; Alison & Dude, for their patience, good humour and being who they are; Sarah, Chris and the girls; Pauline Weston; Nick Duncan; Sue Moorcroft; Neil, for asking and Carrie, for being so lovely; Rosie Heeley, who walked with me; Jim Mcleod; Peter Mark May; Lisa Jenkins; Jonathan Litchfield; Shelley Wilson and my pre-readers - David Roberts, Steve Harris, Wayne Parkin, Katrina Owens Soutar , Kim Talbot Hoelzli, Vix Kirkpatrick, Phil Sloman, James Everington - who steered me right.

STORMBLADE PRODUCTIONS

One

Something covered her face, pressing against her nostrils
and mouth. Fingertips brushed her cheeks and hands
clasped around her neck, thumbs pressing into her
windpipe. Her eyes snapped open and Dale's face filled
her vision, snarling at her, his teeth gritted. She grabbed for
his hands, tried to pull his thumbs away even as darkness
clouded the edge of her sight. Stars, pure white and high
above his head, shone brightly before quickly fading.

STORMBLADE PRODUCTIONS

Two

Polly Harper woke with a start, jerking in her seat and dropping the paperback book that'd been balanced in her lap.

She looked around but the few people who were sitting in the departures lounge with her were otherwise occupied - reading, listening to music, drinking coffee, none of them looking at the potentially crazy woman who was now reaching down to pick up the book from between her feet.

"Bloody hell," she said and breathed in deep. That had been scary. She glanced at her watch, grateful to see she'd only dozed for a few minutes and checked the departures board to make sure her flight was on time. It was still listed to fly at 6am, which gave her half an hour. She'd been at the airport since 4.30, when she breezed through customs,

STORMBLADE PRODUCTIONS

drank a large coffee from the Starbucks booth, resisted the temptation to buy a butter croissant and found a seat where she could see the board clearly. Her book, a new cozy mystery by her favourite writer, had been good, but tiredness had overcome her.

She rolled her neck on her shoulders then rubbed the back of it. A woman sitting across from Polly dipped her newspaper and offered a sympathetic smile.

"Not comfortable, are they?"

"Not really."

Before she went back to her paper, the woman said, "Your phone was beeping while you slept."

"Oh, thanks," said Polly and took it out of her handbag. A missed call and two messages, all from Dale, so she deleted them and put the phone back. She got up, waited

STORMBLADE PRODUCTIONS

for the kinks to work their way out of her thighs and went
to buy some Euros.

It was a bitter irony that, had it not been their
anniversary, Polly wouldn't have gone home at lunchtime
to finish her packing. The plan was they would meet at
home after work, drive to Luton Airport, have a meal in the
departures lounge and catch the late flight to Barcelona.
She didn't like the city, but Dale did and, to be honest, she
couldn't be bothered to argue. They'd been to Barcelona
before. It was lovely the first few visits, but she'd seen Las
Ramblas, she'd been up to the Olympic village, she'd had
cocktails in the W and been accosted by the flower sellers
on the Port Olympic. She hadn't been to Paris though, a
city she'd read and dreamed about since her teens; the city
of eternal love, of narrow alleys and grand gestures, of

wonderful architecture and dark haired men, of fantastic food and jazz cafes. Dale went twice a year with work and didn't like the city at all. "It's like London," he told her once, "but you can't understand the graffiti." She could. She'd taken a night school class in basic French and taught herself further online.

She'd known something was amiss as soon as she pulled into the close and saw his car on the drive - he never came home during the day. She pulled up and let herself quietly into the house.

Dale was upstairs and he wasn't alone. Polly could hear a woman's voice, gasping and grunting.

It felt like she'd been punched in the stomach, leaving her gasping for breath and her throat seemed to close around the large lump that had nestled in it. Not today, of all days. To find out your husband of almost twenty years was having an affair was bad enough, to find out the day before your anniversary was just rubbing salt in the wound.

"No," she said quietly, her palms clammy as she started up the stairs, "it's a mistake." Even as she said it, she knew it was silly - what did she expect to find? Dale and a female companion moving furniture? Maybe his anniversary surprise was to re-do the bedroom.

Three steps from the top, the unseen woman cried, "Oh Dale, that's the fucking spot!"

There must have been anger but she didn't feel it, her movements unhurried as muscle memory got her from the top of the stairs to the bedroom door. She could hear them now, the slap of flesh-on-flesh, the dampness of union, the hurried gasps and sighs.

Polly pushed the door open wide.

The curtains were half drawn, clothes strewn on the ottoman. The lovers were on the bed, the woman on top. She looked young, her skin soft and smooth, her buttocks rounded but firm as they slapped against Dale's thighs, which suddenly seemed much older and saggier than Polly remembered.

They were building to a crescendo as Polly walked into the room. Dale had his eyes closed, his face set in that 'I'm trying not to come' expression Polly hated, as he pawed the girl's big tits. Much bigger tits than Polly had, with dark nipples. The girl had her hands on Dale's chest, her head dropped forward, her fringe over her eyes.

What did this young woman see in him? Polly wondered.

"You bastard," she shouted, and the girl looked around quickly, her eyes suddenly wide, her jaw dropping.

STORMBLADE PRODUCTIONS

"Shit."

Polly didn't go to Barcelona. She walked out, leaving her cheating husband and hollow marriage behind, taking only the case she'd already packed - everything else could wait. She went to a coffee shop, booked the earliest possible flight to Paris, browsed TripAdvisor until she found a hotel she liked the look of and booked that too. Not having anywhere to stay that night, she drove to the airport, checked into the Holiday Inn there and went for a meal.

It was all so easy. And being so proactive helped dampen the pain burning in her chest.

Three

The plane was half-full.

"Good morning," said the Flight Attendant as she checked the boarding ticket and directed Polly a third of the way up the plane.

A man was in the aisle seat of her row and Polly stopped at his side. When it was obvious his attention wasn't going to be diverted from the book he was reading, she said, "Excuse me, can I get by?"

He looked up slowly, his glance taking in her legs, belly and chest, and by the time he reached her face he was smiling. "Hello," he said, his voice just the wrong side of oily.

"I have the window seat," she said.

He made a fuss of having to put his tray away. "Of course," he said and stood up, making a bowing gesture as he did. Tall and thin-faced, he looked very dapper. He wore a charcoal grey three-piece suit, the waistcoat of which had its bottom button undone, onyx cufflinks and a well knotted tie. She smiled, edged to her seat and sat down.

"Let's hope nobody sits between us," he said as he settled back.

"There weren't many people queuing," she said, trying to be polite but hoping a conversation wouldn't develop. On first impression, she didn't like him. Although she hadn't been as blatant in checking him out as he had been, she could see his clothes were a little too tight, as if he didn't want to admit to ageing and middle-age spread, while the grey that poked through the hair colouring at his temples backed it up. Maybe his marriage had broken down too and this was his way of starting again, making himself anew.

"If it's almost empty," he said, offering her a wide smile, "it'll give us a chance to get to know each other."

She almost laughed but bit it back. He was in his early fifties, not much older than her, so why did he think those cheesy lines would work? "I'm tired," she said, "I think I'm going to sleep."

He looked at her and briefly squinted. She wondered where he kept his glasses. "Really?"

"Really."

He shrugged, looking towards the front of the plane. "Suit yourself."

Polly put her bag between her feet, took out her book then slipped off her shoes.

"So what're you reading?"

Sighing, Polly held the book up so he could see the cover.

"The Vauxhall Bridge Mystery?" he said, frowning.

"It's a cozy mystery," she said.

"A what?"

"Cozy. Female sleuth, not too much sex and violence, good fun."

"Ah," he said and held up his book - a pristine copy of the latest Dan Brown. "I prefer this kind of thing."

"I'm sure."

"Uh huh," he said and cleared his throat, as if playing for time while he thought of something to say. "I'm off to a meeting. Business travel is meant to be so glamorous, but it's all airports, aircraft, anonymous meeting rooms and equally anonymous hotel rooms." He smiled, clearly trying to be charming, but it came across as creepy rather than friendly. Mr Creepy, she decided, that suited him perfectly and when she didn't respond, it seemed to throw him. "So are you off to Paris for business or pleasure?"

"Pleasure," she said, "it's our anniversary and I'm joining my husband at the Eiffel Tower. He's in a meeting somewhere, but then we're having a nice romantic weekend."

Something changed in his eyes. "I hope you have a nice time," he said and opened his book. Polly smiled and did the same.

The plane was still taxiing when the first telephones began chiming with incoming messages and passengers got to their feet to pull their belongings from the overhead lockers. Nobody had sat between Polly and the man, and she'd noticed him giving her furtive looks throughout the flight, mainly at her legs. Horrible creepy man.

She waited until he got up and retrieved his laptop case and a small rucksack before she moved across the seats. He looked down and gave her a sour smile. "Enjoy Paris," he said.

"I'll enjoy my romantic weekend," she said.

"I'm sure you will," he said and pushed into the line of people.

Polly watched until he'd left the plane before she stood and waited for someone to let her into the queue.

She went through passport control quickly, the immigration staff apparently uninterested by blonde English women. The man behind the counter quickly checked her photograph then handed the document back with a curt, "Thank you."

"Merci," she said and offered him a bright smile. His expression didn't change.

Charles DeGaulle airport was light and airy, with high ceilings, plenty of glass and pale marbled floors. It wasn't overcrowded and Polly allowed herself to be carried along with the knot of fellow passengers to Arrivals. Some bags had already come onto the carousels and she stood to one side, trying to spot Mr Creepy but he was nowhere to be seen. Ahead, through the windows, she could see roads and car-parks and the sun struggling to break through the clouds.

After she got her case, Polly made her way to the entrance, checking signs and trying to read the language rather than look at the symbols. She passed a couple of small cafes, the smell of fresh coffee intoxicating. Further on was a big restaurant, surprisingly full, and kids dragged their parents into a McDonalds franchise next door. Between the two was a toilet, and she went in, relieved herself, washed her hands and stared in the mirror.

The forty-four-year-old Polly Harper who stared back looked better than she'd expected. Yes there were perhaps a few too many laugh lines around her mouth and eyes but she'd earned and wore them well. Her straight blonde hair was cut to her shoulders and looked good, the fringe covering most of her forehead. She had a narrow nose, blue eyes that seemed darker in winter than summer and thin lips, none of which she particularly liked but all of which made her Polly. She'd never really considered herself pretty but now, looking at herself in the mirror and disconcerted by the vaguely haunted look in her eyes, she realised she would have to or else she'd crumble. What she'd discovered at home, what she'd walked in on, didn't reduce her - if that was the view she took, she was lost. No, she was as pretty as she'd ever been, if she wasn't prettier than she was yesterday or the day before that, and she needed to keep that in the forefront of her mind, to try and drive away the haunted look.

She saw the girl, her eyes large with surprise and perhaps fear. She saw Dale's hands all over her tits and felt a shiver run down her spine - no, don't think about it. It can't be changed now is the time to move forward. Think ahead, think positive. She was here in Paris. So what if she was on her own, she might have been in Barcelona now with a husband she didn't know was cheating on her.

STORMBLADE PRODUCTIONS

Polly ordered a coffee from a busy stand near the main entrance. Next to it was a newsagent and she glanced at the headlines as she waited for her Americano to cool. The police, apparently, were no nearer to finding out the identity of the so-called Necktie Murderer, having just released a suspect.

She blew on the coffee and took a sip - strong and rich, just as she liked it. Now what? She hadn't planned beyond this point and couldn't decide between catching a train into the city, which would be more glamorous, or a taxi, which would be more direct.

She looked up as Mr Creepy came out of the toilet, stopped by the door and used his handkerchief to wipe the corners of his mouth. Surprised, Polly stepped back behind a pillar and counted to five, then peeped around. He was looking in the opposite direction, towards the signs for the train station and that made up her mind on how to get into the city.

Mr Creepy turned slowly and locked eyes with her. A small smile played at the corners of his lips and he nodded. "I see you," he mouthed.

Startled, it felt like his words had pulled the oxygen from her lungs as her heart seemed to thud against her ribs. She slipped behind the pillar again and rested her head against it, her mouth suddenly dry, the only sound the rushing blood in her ears. Had he really mouthed that? Perhaps he was trying to be flirty, a kind of "peekaboo, I see you" and not something sinister, but it hadn't felt like that.

"You're being paranoid," she said out loud as if making a sound would confirm it. Nobody paid her any attention, which didn't help.

STORMBLADE PRODUCTIONS

Not wanting to see what Mr Creepy was doing, she grabbed her case and made for the main doors, trying to lose herself in the gaggle of people there. She didn't turn, didn't pause, just barged her way through and out into the cool morning air.

A few people were standing at the taxi rank but there were more vehicles than passengers so she stopped by the driver's door window of the first unoccupied one.

"Are you free?" she asked the driver, a huge black man who spilled over his seat onto the centre console.

He looked at her and frowned, his lip curling. "Que dis-tu?"

Her mind wouldn't think straight, couldn't translate. She bit her lip, her eyes roving as if trying to find the answer written on the underside of a concrete overpass. "Es-tu libre?"

STORMBLADE PRODUCTIONS

The driver nodded and smiled. His left canine was capped in silver. "Oui, je suis entrer."

"Merci," she said and got into the back, sitting behind him. As he pulled into the traffic, shouting heartily at a bus that wouldn't let him by, Polly risked a glance behind but couldn't see Mr Creepy. She took a deep breath, willing her heart rate to slow down.

The driver tilted his head towards the back seat. "Où voulez-vous aller madame?"

He spoke almost too quickly for her to translate but she heard "aller" and that was enough. Where did she want to go? "Pour L'Hôtel Truffaut s'il vous plaît."

He didn't move his head. "Es-tu sûr?"

Her mind didn't process his question quickly enough. He repeated himself and she frowned, shrugging her

STORMBLADE PRODUCTIONS

shoulders. "Money," he said in English, his accent thick. "Lot money."

She knew it was a long journey and asked how much.

He shrugged with his lips. "Peut être quatre-vingt euro."

It took her a moment to translate - eighty euros seemed a bit steep but it was nearing rush hour. "Oui, c'est bon."

"Tres bien," he said with another smile and pressed a button on the meter. After turning up the radio, he pulled a toothpick from a case that had been squashed into the empty cigarette lighter holder and chewed it as he drove with abandon into the morning traffic.

The drive to Notre Dame took an hour, the driver's language louder and ever more vociferous as he fought for space on roundabouts. On at least two occasions, Polly was convinced there would be a collision, but he always managed to find a bit of space to put the taxi and keep them accident free.

The route showed her a humdrum Paris - she thought briefly of Dale's dismissive graffiti comment - until they turned right onto Quai Saint-Bernard and there was the back of the cathedral. It looked bigger and far more impressive than she thought it would.

"Notre Dame," he said with a sense of pride, "Fifth Arrondissement."

"Merci," she said, her smile wide. She'd wanted to visit the left bank since discovering, in her teens, Henry Miller and Anais Nin, Matisse and Wharton, Satre and F. Scott Fitzgerald, imagining herself in the lives of the bohemians. As real life intruded it had become less of a beacon, but now, wanting to strike out on her own, it made sense. This was her part of Paris, somewhere she could explore and claim as her own. The first of many such things, she hoped.

"You have good time," the driver said nodding.

"Absolument," she said, and he grinned widely at her in the rear view mirror.

He pulled onto Rue Saint-Jacques and soon stopped outside the Hotel Truffaut.

"Mademoiselle," he said, looking over his shoulder. Polly looked at the meter - €72.50.

She got out, paid him eighty euros and told him to keep the change. He smiled, executed a quick three-point turn, flipped off someone who honked their horn and was gone by the time she turned to face the hotel.

Built as part of the Haussmann renovations, with Lutetian limestone blocks to the façade, two large windows stood guard either side of the double-width front door, with three narrow windows on the floor above. The next four floors all had balconies in front of the windows, the ironwork dark blue and offset with pots of colourful flowers that were attached to it.

The reception area was flooded with light from the big windows. Cosy but modern, the walls were pale and crowded with framed pictures, overstuffed leather seats were set out at random and the carpet was thick and dark. A friendly looking woman stood behind the counter at the far end of the space, and she looked up as Polly approached.

"Bonjour, madame, ca va?"

"Bonjour, je m'appelle Polly Harper. I booked a room for the weekend."

"Oh yes, Mrs Harper," said the receptionist without a trace of an accent, "of course." She signed Polly in and gave her a keycard. "You're in room 403, fourth floor. Do you need help with your luggage?"

"No thank you," said Polly, "I just have this case."

"If you need anything else, please ring. Breakfast is between seven and ten."

"Merci."

The receptionist smiled. "De rien."

Polly used the stairs. The fourth floor was quiet and looked plush and expensive. Her room was compact and modern, the air conditioning humming. To her left was the bathroom; ahead the main room which was dominated by a wide double-bed. A desk-cum-dressing table lined the wall across from it.

"Ah," she said as she dropped her handbag and case on the floor, turned and fell onto the bed, "Paris!" She kicked off her shoes, put her arms over her head and stared at the ceiling, smiling. Not how she'd imagined her first time here, but now was the perfect time to clear her mind and focus on a long weekend all to herself in this strange city. She rolled onto her left and looked out of the window, seeing an array of rooftops and the splendid architecture of what looked like a church. She would Google it later, but now it was time to explore.

STORMBLADE PRODUCTIONS

<u>Four</u>

Armed with a tourism pamphlet from reception, Polly stood in front of the hotel and looked at her watch. It was a little after ten. The morning was warm, the sky now almost cloudless and the air smelled of baking. She checked the guide and got her bearings. The Rue Saint-Jacques was alive with people; tourists headed to the cathedral or away from it, wearing hats and t-shirts bearing the Notre Dame logo, mingling with Parisiennes who moved with purpose, carrying briefcases or laptop bags.

A group of children went by, giggling as their teachers shepherded them on, admonishing them if they let go of the hand of their partner. They were followed by a large party of Japanese tourists who all talked at once, none of them listening to the exasperated looking guide who was talking about the street.

Polly fell into step behind them, listening to the guide, and it didn't take long to reach the crossroads at the end of the street. Across the river and a few hundred yards away, Notre Dame Cathedral was an imposing sight: the towers bigger than she'd expected, the Rossetta Window even more glorious. It was everything that she'd hoped it would be and more, and she felt something swell in her chest.

The tourists took pictures until the guide rallied and led them across the road, which they crossed without looking. Car horns blared and angry cyclists shouted to no effect. Polly stayed put; the crossroads was ridiculously busy and she didn't fancy taking her life in her hands.

The smell of coffee drifted to her from the Hotel Notre Dame brasserie and, tempted by the rich aroma, she headed towards the door. Inside was calm and dimly lit, with only a few tables occupied. After getting quickly served at the counter, she sat at one of the window tables. A young waiter brought her drink on a tray - a tall cafetiere and a small delicate cup - and left the receipt on a saucer. She checked it when he'd gone, put the cash down, then poured her coffee and looked out at the morning. Another group of Japanese tourists went by, taking pictures before heading across the bridge opposite. One tourist stopped in the middle of the crossroads to get a better angle for his photograph and a cyclist tapped him on the head as she went by.

The coffee was so good that Polly stayed for another cafetiere, reading her guide and making plans. Having decided to walk to the Louvre, she noticed a smaller street that would take her to the Place Saint Michel and thought that might be more adventurous. She walked back towards the hotel as far as the Jardin Notre Dame café and turned right into Rue de la Huchette.

It was narrow, a canyon hemmed in by five storey buildings, the ground level premises a combination of shops, takeaway booths and restaurants. A Greek tavern, a pizzeria, a cocktail bar; a classy French restaurant, an Italian restaurant and a crepes stand that had clearly seen better days. There were no cars but plenty of people, and she walked, looking around and trying to take everything in, giving way to people who clearly had somewhere to be simply because she didn't. This was how she'd always imagined exploring Paris, at her own pace, following her own interest, taking delight in the architecture and the people and the speed of a life so different - and yet so similar - to her own. When she reached the Place Saint Michel it was almost a disappointment the canyon was finished, though the bright sunlight made up for that.

A kiosque a journax was in the centre of the pavement, its billboard covering the Necktie Murderer. Polly considered picking up a copy of the paper but decided against it; she didn't really want to read about death and destruction. Instead, she crossed the road in front of the Fontaine Saint-Michel, turned left onto Quai des Grands Augustins and crossed to the river side of the street to catch the sunshine. An old man stood by a traffic bollard, smoking, and he smiled as she passed. She smiled back, said "Bonjour" and looked over the wall onto the Seine. There was a walkway below, with tourists and locals and a small group of teenagers sitting in a circle smoking cigarettes. Ahead, a man sat in a deckchair reading a

STORMBLADE PRODUCTIONS

paperback next to a green wooden stall filled with books, maps and magazines.

The view made her smile. Whenever she saw pictures of the Seine, there was always an image of *les bouquiniste,* the fabled used-book dealers. She browsed the stall, found a couple of paperbacks with garish, pulp fiction covers and bought them, smiling broadly at the man in the deck chair who only offered the slightest of smiles in return.

She moved to the next stall, bought a small art print of *La tournée du Chat Noir* even though she knew it was corny, then to the next. Some stalls didn't have anything that drew her attention but she looked at them all, and as the *bouquinistes* got older, they seemed to appreciate her smiles more.

On one stall, she found a stash of Agatha Christie paperbacks, Librairie Des Champs-Elysees editions with vivid yellow covers. She picked one at random and handed it to the *bouquiniste*, who could have been anywhere between seventy and one hundred.

"Bonjour!" she said brightly.

"Hello madam," he replied in French, "lovely day."

"Yes, it's lovely."

"Anglais?"

"Yes, is my accent so bad?"

He waved his hand and pursed his lips. "Non, non, vous êtes très jolie, une véritable rose anglaise." She didn't catch all of it - he didn't have all his teeth - but she got the fact that he thought she was pretty like an English rose and that was enough for her. He smiled and stroked her palm with his forefinger when he gave her change.

"Merci, monsieur," she said and moved on.

STORMBLADE PRODUCTIONS

Their exchange gave her a fresh spring in her step. Further down, trees lined the pavement and Polly enjoyed walking through the dappled sunlight as she browsed the wares. Spotting her purchases, the *bouquinistes* were more attentive, but she didn't buy any more and kept walking until she came to the Ponts Des Artes, one of the main things she wanted to see.

She strolled up the stone steps and onto the wooden planking. The bridge was wide, with benches in the middle and a lot of people. Polly turned in a full circle, trying to take everything in.

The bridge of love: the symbol of the romantic heart of the city. Padlocks filled the railings as far as she could see, attached there by lovers, the keys thrown into the Seine as a testament to a thousand love affairs that could never be broken, at least until the council removed them again.

STORMBLADE PRODUCTIONS

And here she stood, on a grand adventure, at this bridge and it all seemed redundant. She was here because her arsehole of a husband couldn't keep it in his pants, because the love that had filled her life for the past twenty or more years had been snuffed out in one tawdry tableau.

Bollocks.

She wanted to appreciate the love-locks, the thought and sentimentality of the concept, but suddenly the area seemed too vast - the bridge, the sky, the Seine below her. Even the people surrounding her didn't help allay that sense of isolation. A group of school-children bustled past, being herded towards the Louvre, laughing and shouting and completely ignorant of what the bridge meant, as they should be.

Halfway across the bridge a couple gestured for her to take a picture with their camera. She obliged them as they kissed with the padlocks to either side of them with Notre Dame in the background then handed back the camera and kept moving. Ahead she could see the entrance to the Louvre Palace, its imposing stance against the blue sky offset somewhat by the gaggle of children in brightly coloured uniforms who were congregating in front of it.

Polly left the bridge and crossed the road. As she reached the other side, she suddenly had the intense feeling of being watched; a tickling sensation at the back of her neck.

She turned, glancing towards the bridge, but there were so many children and couples it was difficult to pick anyone out. She looked from one side of the bridge to the other, at the people on the steps and those waiting to cross the road, but no-one appeared to be watching her.

Polly brushed the back of her neck and tried to convince herself it was nothing but, walking briskly to the archway, she stole a look over her shoulder.

Mr Creepy stood beside one of the lamp-posts on the bridge. She knew it couldn't be, that it was just someone who looked like him, had the same greying hair and wore a charcoal grey three-piece suit, but he startled her and she felt a jolt of adrenalin rush through her veins.

He was looking to his left. Polly ducked behind a pillar, edging around slowly so she could see him and hopefully he couldn't see her. The man looked at the archway, frowned, then looked to his right. Polly stayed still, the worry fading slightly to be replaced by the ridiculous image of herself as the heroine of the mystery she was reading, standing at a busy tourist attraction spying on a man who might or might not be looking for her.

Mr Creepy looked towards the archway and smiled as if he could see her, then walked down the steps. She felt the tingling sensation on her neck again, convinced he would mouth the words "I see you," but he turned left and disappeared from view.

The breath she'd been holding came out in a rush.

"I'm going mad," she said, and a small boy who was standing beside her, dressed in a bright blue uniform, giggled.

Polly smiled at him and walked into the Cour Carrée, the interior courtyard of the Louvre Palace. It was beautiful, but the grandeur, history and noise of the tourists all built up, overwhelming her so she found a spot out of everyone's way to slowly take everything in. This was

Paris, this was what she'd dreamed of, and she'd so overloaded her senses in the past half hour that time seemed to be slowing down.

She took photographs with her phone, knowing none of them would properly capture the scale of the place, and walked towards the centre of the quadrangle to get a better shot, but there were too many tourists around the fountain for her to get close enough. Large groups of schoolchildren had set up camp, sitting down to tuck into packed lunches. She felt her stomach rumble and rubbed it idly then checked the time on her phone, surprised to see it was after twelve-thirty.

She didn't want to head back the way she'd come - there was too much of any new city to see to retrace your steps - so she left the Cour Carrée in the direction of the Rue Di Rivola where the traffic was heavy, the hustle and bustle noisy and the pavements were full of Parisiennes at lunch and tourists shopping.

Polly window-shopped until she found a little charcuterie where she bought a *jambon beurre* - a fresh baguette with ham and butter - and a cup of strong coffee and carried on walking until she reached Square de la Tour Saint-Jacques. All of the benches were taken and more people sat on the grass, so Polly found herself a spot, sat down, opened her coffee and had lunch.

It was perfect.

After she'd finished her lunch and spent a pleasant hour people-watching, Polly headed back to the hotel on a route that led her past the cathedral. There were too many people on the terrace in front of it for her to want to mingle, so she took a few pictures and crossed the bridge, coming full circle to the hotel Notre Dame.

She looked into the brasserie windows as she walked by, thinking of the wonderful coffee, but the hotel bed was calling. If she didn't have a nap, she would flag by early evening and that would be a waste - not that she had anything specific planned other than it wouldn't be spent laying on the bed eating chocolates and watching TV.

She could have stayed at home for that.

Home. Fleeting images of the naked girl astride him.

Lying, cheating bastard.

Polly shivered, pushing the thought from her mind as she walked back to her hotel.

Five

Polly had fallen asleep in moments.

When she woke, the sun cast slanting shadows through the window and it took a moment to get her bearings. She reached for her phone on the night-stand, looked at the display and groaned, annoyed that it was after six and she'd lost her afternoon.

The display also showed she'd received more messages from Dale.

She sat on the edge of the bed, leaning forward and looking at her bare toes in the thick pile of the carpet. She wiggled them and smiled. Who cared she'd lost a chunk of time; she clearly needed the rest and surely now, of all times, everything was about embracing improvisation.

She'd come here on a whim, taken that glorious walking tour on a whim.

She went for a shower.

The phone was ringing when she came out of the bathroom clad in the softest, fluffiest bathrobe she'd ever worn. She checked the display and took a deep breath. Did she really want to talk to him? Why spoil a good day, even if it was obvious from all his texts he wasn't going to stop until they did communicate.

"What?" she said, struggling to keep her voice even.

"Polly?" He sounded surprised. "I didn't think you'd answer."

"Then why ring?"

"Because I need to speak to you." Surprise had shifted into light desperation. "We," he paused, "we need to..." He took a deep breath, coughed. "We need to sort things out."

Polly bit her lip and waited a moment to compose herself. "Sort things out?"

"Yes, we need to sort out what's happening."

"What's happening is that I came home from work and found you in our bedroom - our bedroom, Dale - with some random girl bobbing up and down on your cock."

"That was unnecessary, Pol," he said, after a moment, in a defeated tone.

His words raised sparks of anger deep in her belly. "Unnecessary? No, that was you putting her in our bed, not me calling you out on it."

He took a deep breath. "I understand you're hurt and angry Pol, please, I'm trying to make amends."

Now it was her turn to take a deep breath. "I'm not sure that amends can be made. You've betrayed me, Dale, and made me doubt the last twenty years meant as much as I thought."

"It did, it does. The last twenty years mean everything to me."

"So what about the girl then? How does she fit into all this?"

She heard him blow out his breath. "It's been tough at work, you know that."

"So?" Dale was a Finance Supervisor, responsible for a lot of company money, who'd worked hard to get where he was and sometimes the stresses and pressures were intense, often around this time of the year. "You have strategic planning every year."

"I know, but…"

STORMBLADE PRODUCTIONS

"So who was she?"

"You don't know her."

"I could tell that from what I saw of her, but that wasn't what I asked."

"She's nobody."

The word hit Polly like a slap and she almost recoiled from the handset. "Nobody?" she hissed through gritted teeth. "You threw away twenty years for nobody?"

"No, Pol, that's not what I meant, you know that. She's an intern."

"An intern?" The company was flooded with them as the Strategic Planning time rolled around, and he'd often said how much fun they had winding these kids up.

"Yes." The defeat was clear in his voice, as if he could go no lower. "She didn't mean anything, it was a glitch, I was feeling the pressure and I needed to vent."

STORMBLADE PRODUCTIONS

"And so you chose her?" Something clicked in her mind - the late nights every year, the stresses and anxiety - and sudden realisation hit her. "She wasn't the first, was she?"

His silence told her more than if he'd spoken.

"How many have there been?" More silence, which helped feed the angry sparks. "How many functions have I been to and had these interns introduced to me?"

"Polly…"

"No, tell me. How many times have you introduced me to people without telling me that you were fucking them?"

"Polly, you're getting upset."

"Upset? Dale, you don't seem to grasp what's happening here."

"I do," he said quickly, his voice calm, "I honestly do. You're hurt, you feel betrayed, I get that, I understand. I'm an arsehole, I've hurt you and our marriage but we need to sit down and work things through. I can change, I can make amends but I need you to allow me to do it."

"Can you hear yourself?"

"Yes and it makes sense, we just need to calm ourselves down. I know we can work it out."

She didn't know what to say. It wasn't that she believed him, he was just saying whatever he thought would win her over, but was this simply a stumbling block to overcome? Could she ever see it that way? She closed her eyes, watched herself walk into the bedroom again, saw the girl - the intern - with the perfect arse bobbing up and down and felt a wave of nausea roll over her.

"Have your long weekend in Paris and when you come back we'll talk."

STORMBLADE PRODUCTIONS

"My…" She stopped, frowned. "What do you mean, my long weekend in Paris?"

"Well that's where you are, isn't it?"

She thought of Mr Creepy and his 'I see you'. "How do you know?"

"Because you booked with the credit card. I checked it online at lunchtime."

The anger flooded back. "You checked to see where I was?"

"Of course, I was worried about you."

"Not so worried you couldn't keep yourself out of that girl though, eh?"

"Pol, there's no need for that."

"No." She terminated the call, threw the phone on the bed and stalked back into the bathroom. Some make-up, do her hair, put on that black dress she'd packed to surprise

STORMBLADE PRODUCTIONS

him - ha, what a waste of time that idea was - and go out to enjoy herself in the Parisienne nightlife.

The phone bleeped with a text message but she slammed the bathroom door against the sound.

STORMBLADE PRODUCTIONS

<u>Six</u>

"Very nice," she told her reflection in the full length mirror behind the door.

She didn't go out that often, not enough to get properly dolled up - in fact, the last time had probably been one of Dale's functions, and just thinking about it made her bite back on the rising anger. She smoothed the dress over her belly, teased the hem down her legs a little bit, then stood up straight and tidied the straps at her shoulders.

The little black dress fitted her well, her make-up was understated and she'd brushed and gelled her hair until she was happy.

STORMBLADE PRODUCTIONS

She got her handbag and went down the stairs, the heels on her shoes big enough to accentuate her calves but not vertiginous enough to make her unsteady.

Outside it was a warm evening and she could smell spices and garlic, strong coffee, a multitude of perfumes and cigarette smoke. There were a lot of people around. Couples walked by arm in arm, sometimes looking at one another, sometimes pointing towards the cathedral, all of them consumed with the other. Groups of friends, loud and raucous, on and off the pavement, ignorant of the traffic. People got into and out of taxis; cars dropped friends and loved ones off. She spotted people on their own and wondered who they were on their way to meet, if they were perhaps about to embark on a blind date that would change their lives forever.

STORMBLADE PRODUCTIONS

And what did the evening hold in store for her? She decided to walk up to the brasserie, get a coffee and something to eat and then take the evening as it came. Normally she liked to plan, but now, the thought of not knowing what was going to happen was exhilarating. She had no intention of going to a club, but she might find a kindred spirit in the brasserie and the night was young. She thought of books she'd read, films she'd watched, where a stranger in a strange land talks to people and finds out the secret of life. She didn't expect that to happen, but she might meet someone interesting who could tell her a story or, perhaps, might ask to hear about hers.

Most of the outdoor tables at the brasserie were taken so she went inside. Her waiter from earlier saw her, smiled and nodded towards a small table in the corner that looked out over the crossroad and cathedral. A middle-aged couple were just leaving and putting on light anoraks, the man helping the woman. She offered a gracious smile that didn't touch her eyes and in return he gave a nod that was too curt to be affectionate. Polly watched them, her hand against her throat, and wondered when they'd started being awkward to one another.

Had she and Dale been awkward? Was it something others could see, their friends perhaps, but she couldn't?

The couple said goodnight to the waiter in German and then they were gone. He cleared the table, ushered Polly to sit down as he went away then came back with a glass of water and the menu.

"Madame?" he asked, "comment allez-vous ce soir?"

"Bon," she said, "et vous?"

"Je suis magnifique," he said with a big smile. "Anglais?"

"Oui."

"Always have I wanted to go to London."

"It's a great city, though not as beautiful as here."

He shrugged. "I grew up in Paris, but now I am twenty and want to see the world."

"I'm sure you will. What's your name?"

"Francois."

"Pleased to meet you, Francois," she said and held out her hand. He shook it. "Je suis Polly."

He smiled broadly. "Bonjour, Polly."

She ordered a coffee and he left.

"Excuse me?" The voice, American-accented, was behind her. Polly twisted around and saw a woman in her early thirties with a round, pretty face and dark eyes. Her white-blonde hair was pulled back into a pony tail and she wore a navy blue skater dress. Her legs were tanned and toned and she held a small clutch purse against her belly.

"Yes?"

"I'm real sorry to be a pain in the ass," she said, pointing to the empty seat, "but is anyone sitting there?"

"No."

"Would you mind?" the woman asked, edging around the table. "I'm so grateful. I heard good things about this place but nowhere said it filled up so quickly. I dropped by hoping for the best and spent the last five minutes wandering around trying to figure out what to do, and then I saw you."

"That's fine."

The woman laughed, a delicate sound. "I'm so sorry, I talk too much, I mean, we don't even know one another and here I am, all chatty Kathy and taking over." She sat down and put her purse on the table. "I'm Katrina," she said, holding out her hand.

Polly introduced herself as she shook.

Francois arrived with her coffee, put it down and raised his eyebrows at Katrina. "Do you mind?" she asked.

"No, I was going to grab something to eat anyway."

Katrina turned her attention to Francois. "Another coffee, black, please." When he'd gone, she looked at Polly. "This is very nice of you."

"It's a new me," said Polly, "I'm trying to be more brave."

"Well good for you. I promise I'm not a serial killer or anything."

"I believe you."

"Speaking of which, did you see this business about the Necktie Murderer?"

STORMBLADE PRODUCTIONS

"I saw some headlines, but I don't know much else."

Katrina leaned forward, elbows on the table, her expression suggesting she had vital gossip to impart. "Apparently, someone is bumping off seemingly random people by strangling them and dumping their bodies in the Seine. It's never a tourist, there's no sign of assault or robbery and apparently it's been going on for a while, a couple of victims a year."

"You're kidding. And they don't have any clues?"

"Apparently not. They had a suspect but they've had to let them go. Meantime, the last murder was in April, the body dropped in the river down a ways, near the Pont de Arts bridge."

Although she'd said it gracelessly, Polly knew what she meant. "I was there earlier today, I went for a walk and wanted to see the love-locks."

"Gee, you saw them? I got here two days ago and I've been trying to find a walking tour since."

"I got a pamphlet and walked it myself."

Francois came back with Katrina's coffee. "Are you ready to order?"

"Deux minutes, sil vous plait?" Polly said with a smile and he left.

"What did you say?" asked Katrina when he'd gone.

"To come back in two minutes. Would you care to join me for dinner?"

"I'd love to." She picked up the menu. "If you don't mind me saying, I think trying to be more brave is definitely working for you, going on your own walking tour then asking a stranger to dinner."

"I wouldn't be so brave if I wasn't here on my own."

Katrina nodded. "Getting away or needing your own space?"

"Both."

"Me too. I hit thirty, had a boyfriend who wouldn't commit, a job that paid well but wasn't going anywhere and I was bored. I bit back those feelings until my thirty-second birthday and did a life audit. Same boyfriend, job and lack of commitment and still bored so I shook everything up a little." She put her menu down and offered a tight smile. "Anyway, I'm going to have the Hachis Parmentier, I saw someone eat it last night, it's like a French version of shepherd's pie."

"I'm going to have the Sole Meunière, that looks and sounds lovely."

"A good choice. Do you drink, Polly?"

"I could be tempted."

Francois came back and they ordered.

"And could we have a jug of pastis, please?" asked Katrina, "diluted." She looked at Polly. "It's delicious, a spirit that tastes like aniseed, it'll knock your socks off."

Francois put two plates in the middle of the table, one with tomato bruschetta's, the other with a crock of tapenade and some toast corners. "Amuse bouche," he said.

"Thank you," said Katrina, watching him go. "So young," she said and spread some tapenade on a piece of toast. "Anyway, I'd been putting some money away so I told my boyfriend to take a hike, sold the house and made a tidy profit, quit my job and decided to travel. I'd been to Europe, London mostly, in my teens and it felt like time to explore again." Katrina ate her toast. "I started in Berlin, which was glorious, and worked my way across Germany, but apart from Cologne I didn't enjoy that. I have another week or so here, then I head to Bordeaux for a week, then it's Madrid, Seville and finally Lisbon. After that, who knows. What about you?"

Polly recounted her story as she ate a piece of bruschetta, which was tart and fresh. Katrina spread her toast, her expressions expansive.

"What an asshole," she said when Polly finished telling her about the phone call.

Francois put the jug of pastis on the table and took away the empty plates. Katrina poured two glasses, handed one to Polly and held hers up for a toast.

"Did you ever drink Pernod?"

"Pernod and black," said Polly, "when I was a teenager."

STORMBLADE PRODUCTIONS

Katrina smiled. "Then prepare to relive your teenage years, my friend. Salut!"

Seven

The pastis did remind Polly of her teenage years and it was stronger than she'd expected. Katrina kept their glasses topped up and the meal was consumed - the fish as delicate and delicious as the menu promised - and the plates collected in a blur. Her new American friend was good company, bright and engaging and they talked as if they'd known one another for years. They were considering options for dessert and teasing Francois by not being able to make up their minds when Polly's phone rang. She wasn't surprised when she looked at the display.

"Dale."

"Oh tell that douche to go boil his head," Katrina suggested.

"I will." Polly got up too quickly and her head swam, so she held onto the chair until it settled then went outside. "What do you want, Dale?"

"I wanted to make sure you were okay after our conversation."

"Why shouldn't I be?" He said something but there was a blast of noise, as if from a loudspeaker, that drowned his words. "I can't hear you," she said, bored already.

"Are you tipsy?"

"I might be." She walked around the corner into Rue Saint-Jacques and stood at the kerb. A man in a charcoal grey three-piece suit was standing across the junction, leaning on the bridge abutment and the surprise sobered her slightly, making her heart beat quicken. He had greying hair and was reading a copy of 20 Minutes, his face mostly hidden. Quickly, she moved further down the street.

Dale was still talking. "…that's what I think anyway. What do you reckon?"

"I haven't listened to a word you said."

He offered a nervous laugh. "Come on, what do you want from me?"

Polly stopped in a doorway and risked a glance back at the bridge. The man she'd seen had gone and she breathed a sigh of relief before wondering if he'd ever been there at all. Could it be she'd imagined Mr Creepy over a random commuter making his weary way home? After all, how many charcoal grey suits were there in Paris?

She realised Dale was talking again. "What?" she said, impatiently.

STORMBLADE PRODUCTIONS

"Aren't you listening?" There was another burst of loud talking. "I'm telling you that I want to work it out. I want us to be together. I had a word with Freya today…"

Hearing the name sobered her further. "Dale, for fucks sake, don't name her, I don't want to think of her as a person."

"I told her it's nothing, I'm going back to you."

"Who said that?"

Dale gave an exasperated sigh. "Haven't you been listening to anything…?"

"No, I haven't. I have to go."

"Of course you do," he said, "make sure you enjoy Paris."

She ended the call abruptly and walked back to the corner, scanning across the road in case the man who might have been Mr Creepy had come back. He hadn't so she went into the brasserie, annoyed that the pleasant buzz she'd been building had now been shooed away.

"Hey," said Katrina as she sat down, "everything okay?"

"Fine, except I'm sobering up. How about we go somewhere to drink and dance the night away?"

"I like it, any suggestions?"

"No," said Polly and called Francois over. "Me and Katrina want to go out dancing and drinking, where would you suggest?"

Francois looked at them in turn, smiling. "Me and my friends go to Club Eric. Such *joli* girls as you, that's the place."

"Where is it?" asked Polly.

"Do you know Rue de la Huchette?"

"I do," she said, surprised and pleased.

"Bon, halfway along, you will see it. Good drink, good music."

"Merci beaucoup, Francois," Polly said and kissed him on each cheek.

Eight

Club Eric reminded Polly of her teenage years far more than the pastis had, though she assumed the neon and day-glo paint was used ironically since she was clearly the oldest person in the room. Even the doorman, who'd let them in with no trouble, looked half her age.

The club occupied one floor of a building with a kebab shop at the ground floor and the queue snaked up a narrow stairwell which smelled of doner meat, sex and pot. Inside, the throbbing music - lots of drum machines and synthesisers - vibrated in her ears and feet. Some bistro tables were spread out by the main door, butting up to the dance floor which took up the most space in the room. The bar hugged the left wall and the DJ's booth was on a podium at the far end, only vaguely visible through the flashing lights that backed him. A green laser sporadically shot beams across the low ceiling.

"Loud!" shouted Katrina.

"Get a drink!" Polly shouted back.

Although it was still early the club was packed and Polly had to push past people to get to the bar. When she finally reached it and squeezed into a gap, she saw at least two dozen other hands holding Euros to attract the attentions of the bar staff. It took ten minutes to get served and felt like half as long to fight her way back to the table Katrina had secured.

"Brasserie de Bretagne Britt Blanche?" asked Katrina, examining the bottle.

"They don't do Bud."

Polly sipped her beer and watched the crowd, feeling the urge to dance. She waited for a song she knew - or didn't sound like an out-take from a Jarre album - but didn't recognise any of them. The rest of the clubbers did, crowding out the dance floor and taking up the space between tables.

She let the music rush over her, feeling the beat in her body and moving to it as the inclination took her, surrounded by warm bodies, breathing in the fug of air, sweat, deodorant and magic cigarettes. This was the adventure she'd sought, enjoying herself in a random and slightly tacky bar in the middle of Paris, half-cut and not really sure of what was going on.

"We're being watched," said Katrina, leaning close. "Other side of the room, two guys, can you see them?"

Polly scanned the tables but didn't spot anyone obvious. "No."

"There," Katrina pointed and Polly saw two men look away quickly. "Yes," she said, "got them."

"Wouldn't it be funny if we got propositioned?" asked Katrina and laughed.

Polly smiled. The last song was overtaken by the opening chords of 'Blue Monday'. "I'm going up," she said, "are you coming?"

"I'll look after the drinks."

The exhilaration of dancing kept Polly on the floor for three more songs and when she got back to the table, Katrina was drinking a second bottle of beer and her own had a twin.

"From our admirers," said Katrina.

Polly sat down, took a swig and held the bottle up as a toast. The taller of the two men, who wore a dark suit, nodded and offered a shy smile. He had a long thin face and lots of jet black hair which curled down over his right eye.

"How was the dancing?"

"Brilliant, I haven't felt like this in ages."

A reworked Human League song started, but rather than fight her way back to the floor, Polly danced in her chair and sang along at the top of her voice. When it finished, Katrina leaned forward and held her bottle up. Polly chinked it without thinking.

"Don't look behind you," said Katrina, "but we're being approached."

Polly was aware of someone standing behind her and turned to see the tall man with his striking hair.

"Allo?"

"Bonjour," she said.

STORMBLADE PRODUCTIONS

"Ah, English or Australian?"

"English. Well, I'm English, she's American."

"It is good to meet you," he said and held out his hand. "My name is Manu, this is Antoine."

She introduced herself, glancing briefly at Antoine as he moved around the table towards Katrina but focussing her attention on Manu. He looked even better close up than he had from across the room.

He said her name a couple of times, as if testing how it felt in his mouth. "That's a lovely name."

"Thank you." She wondered how often he tried this charm offensive. "Manu's an interesting name."

"Short for Emanuel. Too much of a mouthful."

"Of course."

"So how did your international friendship begin?"

"We met this evening," Polly said.

STORMBLADE PRODUCTIONS

"Just this evening?" he said, his eyes twinkling.

Polly felt a tingling sensation in her belly. "Yes," she said, "seems to be the night for it."

"Indeed." He grabbed a chair from the next table and pulled it over. "Do you mind?"

"Not at all."

"Merci. So what brings you to my wonderful city?"

"A sense of adventure," she said.

He smiled and she watched his face. His teeth were very white, his lips thin and there was a faint shadow of stubble on his chin and upper lip.

"Adventure in the city of love?"

The corners of his lips raised - was he smirking at her? She didn't want to answer and could imagine sitting with this handsome man talking and sharing drinks and finding herself revealing far too much. "Just adventure," she said finally. "Not because of the city of love."

"You are here alone?"

The same smirk - he wasn't asking because he wanted her life story, he wanted to know the lie of the land. "I'm not."

The words seemed to deflate him. "That is a shame," he said. She didn't like this change and realised with a start that she'd enjoyed the flirting. Less than a day ago, she'd been happily married, and now she was in a tiny nightclub in Paris flirting with a stranger.

"I'm here with a friend," she said and smiled. He smiled back. "Me and a girlfriend," she said, making the lie up as she went, "fancied a weekend away."

"She is not here?"

STORMBLADE PRODUCTIONS

"No, she wanted to go on a bus tour." Did they even do bus tours? Why had she said that?

"She will enjoy it," he said, nodding as if to show he knew she wasn't telling the truth.

"I'm sure," she said, suddenly feeling coy. This wasn't how things were - this wasn't how her life was - she didn't flirt with men she'd just met, she only mingled with men she'd known for years: mutual friends, friends of Dale, husbands of her friends. She felt empowered, frightened and, most of all, alive and realised she liked it.

Antoine leaned across the table. "Drinks?"

"I will have a beer," said Manu.

"Same for me," said Polly.

As Antoine made his way to the bar, a remix of 'Electric Dreams' began playing. "I love this song," Polly said.

Manu leaned forward and put his hand over hers. His skin was warm. "Do you want to dance?"

She liked the pressure of his hand as much as she liked him leaning in to speak. She liked better that he'd asked her to dance.

"I'd love to," she said, raised her eyebrows at Katrina and allowed him to lead her by the hand to the dance floor.

They moved to the music, Polly much more graceful though Manu definitely had the beat. The floor filled, pushing them closer together and a new song started, a slower one Polly didn't recognise. Manu took her hands and tilted his head as he looked at her, trying to gauge if this move was too much - or, perhaps, too little. Polly liked the sensation, liked the attention. More people on the floor, pressing against her back. The music, the beat, the lights, the heat, everything was pushing her towards him. He danced with his back to the DJ, the beam of the laser cutting the air above his head. He pulled her closer, gently, timing each move to the beat so it felt organic, a natural movement neither of them was capable of over-riding. The music moved through her with the alcohol, she felt it expressed through her arms, legs and feet. She closed her eyes, swaying and enjoying the moment. Manu pulled and she opened her eyes, surprised to see him so close. He let go of her hands - she didn't want to release him, tried to hold onto his fingertips with her own - and then he put his hands on her hips.

The touch was an electric charge, shorting between his hands and driving deep into her belly. She closed her eyes again, let him pull her closer and draped her arms over his shoulders.

Another song mixed in, with a faster beat, and Manu moved backwards slightly. Polly let her arms slide from his shoulders reluctantly, smiling at him as she stepped back.

Katrina and Antoine were kissing when they got back to the table. Polly took a big gulp of her beer when she sat down and Manu moved his chair so he was closer to her as he drank half of his. He put his hand on the table next to hers, their little fingers barely touching though she still felt the spark. She liked that he was moving things forward but taking it steady and stroked his finger with her own.

"Our friends," he said, "they look happy."

"They do," she said and drained her beer.

"Would you like to go somewhere for a coffee?"

"That'd be nice," she said.

STORMBLADE PRODUCTIONS

"Good, I know a place."

She got up and walked around the table, leaning close to Katrina and tapping her gently on the shoulder. Katrina seemed reluctant to stop kissing but did, looking at Polly with wide eyes.

"We're going, you be careful."

"Surely, you too."

"Let's meet at the brasserie tomorrow." It suddenly seemed important to Polly they do that, to make sure the other was safe.

"For breakfast or lunch?"

"Both. Stay there until we meet."

Katrina closed her eyes, wrinkled her nose and smiled, then went back to Antoine. Polly accepted Manu's outstretched hand and he led them out of the club.

Rue de la Huchette was buzzing with music and conversation, groups of people standing in front of bars and restaurants or making their way from one end to the other. The narrow strip of sky she could see above, sandwiched between the building tops like an architectural letterbox, was a pale purple. Looking up made her feel giddy for a moment and she couldn't tell if she was tipsy because the beer was stronger or if she'd had more than she thought.

"This way," said Manu, guiding her towards the cathedral. "Are you okay?"

Was she? She blinked, tried to think. "Yes," she said finally and squeezed his hand, "I am."

At the end, Manu turned right, but Polly stole a glance at the cathedral and noticed, with a moment of shocking clarity, someone standing at the kerb looking towards the hotel brasserie. She felt a chill pinch the skin across her shoulders.

"Dale?" she said, though the man was too far away to hear her. She stopped, her hand sliding from Manu's as he kept walking. He turned, frowned at her.

"What is it?"

Polly stepped to the kerb, straining her eyes. The man - she knew it was Dale, as ridiculous as that sounded - was just far enough away that she couldn't be certain. She felt Manu's hand on her elbow and tried to shake him off.

"No," he said as she stepped into the road. A car swerved and honked its horn, shocking her back onto the path. Manu grabbed her arms, holding her upright and turned her to face him.

"What was that?" he asked.

"Nothing," she said, "I…" She turned, but the man - Dale - was gone. "I thought I saw someone, that's all."

"Too many people to see some one," he said, smiling. He started to walk and Polly allowed herself to be led, waiting for her shoulders to relax. It couldn't be Dale, that was ridiculous, like seeing Mr Creepy earlier on - she was putting faces on strangers now. Perhaps it was delayed shock at the stressful situation? She wondered if it was easily dealt with, perhaps by having a nice time with Manu and drinking a little more than she should.

The Café Léaud occupied a corner a few hundred yards from the L'Hotel Truffaut. They took one of the bistro tables at the front and Manu went inside to get their drinks. Left alone, Polly stretched her arms then rubbed the back of her neck. The dancing had done her the world of good and, the shock of seeing Dale (or not) aside, she felt brighter than she had in the past twenty-four hours. She checked her mobile and saw three texts, all from him, which she deleted without reading. She put her phone away as Manu came back and, in the harsher light of the café windows, she realised he was only in his mid-thirties.

She bit her lip, looked towards the pavement. What did she expect to happen here and was it what she wanted? Or even what he wanted? If she could see that he was probably ten years younger than her then he, no doubt, could see the same.

"I decided against coffee." He sat down and put a tray on the table between them. "The night is yet young, I think beer is still in order." He handed her a stemmed glass with a rich brown liquid in it.

"Thank you," she said.

STORMBLADE PRODUCTIONS

He held up his glass and waited for her to touch hers to it. "To a lovely evening."

That first beer went down so well, Manu got two more. They talked, sometimes in French but mostly in English, of everything and nothing, not divulging personal details but skirting around the edges, giving clues and leaving hints.

More people appeared, walking with purpose into the night. Horns blared. Somebody shouted and she heard running feet. The tables around them filled, the noise level increasing, friendly chatter that sounded warm and welcoming.

And all the while, Manu either talked or listened - his face animated always. Out here, he was more handsome than the lighting in the club had allowed, his black hair thick. The five o'clock shadow was growing ever darker and his eyebrows were smudges above piercing brown eyes that never glanced away from her face. His nose had an interesting kink just above the tip and she wondered what it would feel like to kiss it.

Did she want to kiss it? Was that where this heading? Polly took a deep sip of her beer. Yes, that was where this was heading - she wanted to kiss the kink in his nose, she wanted to kiss his cheeks, feel his thin lips against her own. He lifted his glass and she watched his wide hand and long fingers. How would they feel caressing her cheek, her arms, her chest, her body?

It wasn't about Dale and it wasn't about revenge, it was what she wanted to happen next.

Later, Manu looked at his watch. "It's not evening anymore," he said, his words softly slurring.

STORMBLADE PRODUCTIONS

"So what now?" she asked, aware her own words slurred. She knew what she wanted to say, but didn't know if she had the courage to say it.

"I do not know, Polly. You are the guest in my city, what you want?"

"How about a nightcap? My hotel isn't far from here."

He smiled and she knew. He was so devilishly handsome…

STORMBLADE PRODUCTIONS

<u>Nine</u>

"Here we are," she said, feeling a little foolish and light-headed, like a teenager who knows tonight is the night.

"Ah," said Manu, standing so close she could smell his aftershave. He cupped her left buttock.

"Yes," she said and opened the door with the passkey. Sliding his hand up to the small of the back, Manu propelled her into the room and kissed her before the door had even closed. He pressed her to the wall, his lips hungry against hers, their tongues playing. He ran his hands up and down her sides but didn't touch her breasts though she desperately wanted him to. Their breathing quickly became hard and heavy.

He slid his hand down her belly and even through the fabric of her dress it left a burning sensation against her skin. It had been a long time since anyone other than Dale had kissed or touched her like this and she liked it: the new sensations, the heightened feelings, the total abandonment that came with kissing a stranger in a foreign city.

"Bed?" he said, barely breaking the kiss.

"Through there," she murmured, kissing between words.

Manu wrapped his arms around her waist and lifted her off the ground. She squealed, kicked off her shoes and wrapped her legs around him as he carried her into the main area and put her on the bed.

"You're so pretty," he said, propping himself up on his arms. She unbuttoned his shirt and a necklace, a small silver Algerian loveknot, hung down. She reached for his face, wanting to kiss him again but he stood up, shrugged off his jacket and dropped it on the floor.

He grasped the hem of her dress and pulled it up over her body and head. She raised her arms to allow it and he kissed the inside of her elbow, tracing down the inside of her upper arm with his fingertips. She felt the shiver run all the way through her. He kissed her mouth, pushing her back against the bed, and the animalistic nature of the move took her by surprise.

Manu kissed a trail across her cheek and nibbled on her earlobe, which sent sparks through her veins. He brushed her neck lightly with his nose and lips and she groaned, tilting her head to give him better access. Understanding completely, he nuzzled behind her ear and she squirmed, slipping her hands into his shirt. His chest was smooth, his nipples hard, and she stroked her fingernails up his abs. It was his turn to groan and he nipped at her neck, little bites that excited her even more.

He stood and pulled off his shirt. She tried to move with him, wanting his touch, wanting to touch but he pushed her back, a little rougher than she'd expected. She liked it. He looked, brazen in his appreciation of her and she felt embarrassed under his gaze - only Dale had seen her like this, breathing heavy and wearing only her bra and knickers, for a long time. She put her right arm over her breasts and tried to cross her legs, angling her left arm over her groin. He smiled, reached down, cupped her right ankle and lifted her leg.

He looked at her foot and licked her sole from heel to toes. Another new sensation to make her squirm, it felt exquisite and she wanted him to do it again.

"Did you like that, ma cherie?"

STORMBLADE PRODUCTIONS

"Yes," she said, her voice sounding too deep, "do it again."

"Plus tard," he said and knelt down, kissing his way up her calf and licking the crease of her knee. She liked it, was content to drown in the pleasure, but she was on edge too and that seemed to heighten her sexuality. She wasn't uncomfortable, not really, but with him paying such close attention, she remembered seeing him in the light of the café. Did her legs look alright? When had she last shaved? Would he be mentally comparing her to women his own age?

He kissed up her leg, swatting her protective hand away when he reached the top of her thigh. Moving forward on the bed he spread her legs.

"De toute beauté," he said, staring at her knickers as he traced two fingers down the front panel. She groaned, deep in her throat, and he pressed harder, then stroked towards her inner thighs, making her groan again.

He brushed his mouth over her knickers and she felt the warmth of his breath on her skin. He shifted, his lips touching just above the line of her knickers, and worked towards her stomach, kissing her navel, teasing it with his nose, dipping his tongue in.

He moved further, his chest pressing against her groin, and slid his hands over the cups of her bra. Deftly, he reached under and unclipped it, pushing it up. His hands covered each breast and he rubbed his palms gently over her nipples.

She looked down, watching him between the cleavage he'd created as he held her breasts. His necklace dipped against her skin with every move he made. She watched his lips kiss a trail upwards, watched his hands move over her breasts, his fingers digging into the giving flesh.

His hot groin was now pressed against her own and she could feel his hardness. She reached for it, caressing him through his trousers and making him groan in turn as she undid the clasp and unzipped the fly. He teased her left nipple, then her right as she pushed his trousers past his buttocks. With a sudden move, he sucked on her breast, pressing his teeth against the delicate flesh as if to leave a love-bite, to mark his territory.

Then he was on the bed, moving so he straddled her, and put his hands on her chest, rubbed them up to her shoulders and back before sliding them to the base of her neck. He leaned down, kissing her again, his tongue searching out hers. He groaned, she groaned, he pressed his hands against her neck. Nobody had ever kissed her while squeezing her neck and, again, she liked the roughness of it.

She kissed him back hard, her hands around his waist, trying to pull him tighter against her.

STORMBLADE PRODUCTIONS

Ten

The room was grey.

She was on her side, looking towards the window, the curtains half drawn to let in the curious light. Licking her lips, she shifted around and sat on the edge of the bed, her head clanging with the movement. She pressed fingertips to both temples and squeezed her eyes shut until the pounding ceased. Slowly opening her eyes, she saw her clothes were strewn across the room.

She suddenly remembered Manu and turned her head carefully. He wasn't in bed. She stood, walked to the window and looked out at a blanket of fog that hung over the rooftops.

With a groan, she turned away. Where was he, what time was it? She picked up her watch from the bedside table and saw it was early afternoon.

"Shit."

A note lay on the other pillow and she picked it up. *Ma cherie* was written in a neat, sloping script on the back and she unfolded it.

You were sleeping so peacefully when I had to leave, though be assured I kissed you as I went. Thank you for last night, I hope to see you again. Love always, Manu.

There was a line of x's and he'd written his mobile number below them.

Polly stretched and wondered if Katrina had waited for her in the brasserie, then went for a shower.

STORMBLADE PRODUCTIONS

Turning down the water temperature until it was almost cold had shocked away a lot of last night's grogginess. Parts of her ached that hadn't ached in years but she savoured the feeling, though she was surprised at the bruises on her arms, and her throat felt sore.

She dressed quickly - jeans, t-shirt, trainers - and rushed downstairs. The man on reception, who she'd not seen before, ignored her as she passed. Outside the fog was lowering and the day looked greyer than it had through her window. There were a few people around but noise was muffled, as if dampened by the weather conditions.

She walked as quickly as she could, dodging people who stopped in her path, stepping onto the road when the pavement was too busy. The cathedral looked too far away, diffused in the poor light.

STORMBLADE PRODUCTIONS

None of the tables were outside at the brasserie and for one awful moment she thought it was closed, then she noticed someone moving inside. As she passed the windows, she peered in trying to see if Katrina was in there. A lot of empty tables dotted the room.

Inside was quiet, with only the slightest hum of conversation. Polly walked to the counter and waited for the waiter at the till to turn to her.

"Oui?" he asked, his expression one of complete disinterest.

"Is Francois working today?"

The waiter frowned. "Quoi?"

"Francois?" She tried to think of the French. "Travail? Jour de travail?"

"François ne fonctionne pas ici."

It took her a moment to figure it out. "He does work here, he served me yesterday."

"Non."

Polly made a frustrated sound in her throat and looked around at the patrons but couldn't see Katrina amongst them. She checked the toilets but they were empty. She found another waiter who she vaguely recognised from yesterday.

"Excuse moi," she said and waited, again, for him to take his time turning around. "I came in yesterday, met an American woman. Have you seen her?"

"Non," he said, looking through her, "I do not know who you mean."

Annoyed and starting to feel frustrated, Polly left the brasserie. The fog had had brought the sky lower and she could taste moisture in the air.

Where could Katrina be? Polly couldn't remember if she'd mentioned a hotel, didn't know of anywhere she planned to go. But she had to be somewhere and Polly realised she could investigate - rather than reading about a plucky woman sleuth, she could become one.

She would try the Rue de la Huchette again; beyond that was her path from yesterday, the walking tour Katrina had seemed so excited by.

As Polly walked, the fog now below the level of the roofs and the moisture collecting on her eyelashes, she had the sensation of being watched. At the corner, she stopped and turned slowly. Mr Creepy was across the road, leaning against a wall with his arms folded across his chest. He smiled broadly and mouthed, "I see you."

Fear jolted her, pulling her shoulders and sending sharp pains into her fingertips. She backed into the wall, struggling to breathe. Mr Creepy kept smiling, not moving. Polly edged sideways, trying to find the corner. Where was it?

Mr Creepy nodded and she watched his mouth form "I see you," but this time, even over the road noise, she thought she heard it.

Finding the corner, she ran into Rue de la Huchette, not looking back. The fog was drifting through the narrow street, curling against the upper storey windows, tendrils reaching to the ground. Most of the restaurants and take-aways were closed, and the people around her looked closed too, avoiding each other's gazes.

Ahead she saw the kebab shop, the same doorman as last night standing on the pavement, eating a sandwich.

"Hello!" she called, "bonjour!"

He watched her, still eating until she stood in front of him, trying to catch her breath. "Do you remember me?" she asked.

The doorman shrugged, ate more of his sandwich. Some meat from it gathered at the corner of his mouth.

"Do you understand me?" she asked, willing her breathing to calm down. "Comprenez-vous?"

"Oui."

"I don't know the French, do you remember me?"

"Oui."

"Thank you, what about the girl I was with?"

He took another big bite of his sandwich. More meat fell to the ground. "Oui, American."

"Yes, have you seen her?"

"Polly?"

His voice was all she heard, carried by the eddying fog. She tried to take a deep breath but couldn't and the fog got denser as she slowly turned.

"Polly, it is you," said Dale. He was wearing his navy blue suit and black loafers, his white shirt unironed, his tie askew. Two days growth of stubble lined his jaw. "I thought I'd lost you."

"What are you doing here?" she asked, gulping in moist air. "How did you find me?"

He pulled her into a tight embrace, pressing her head against his shoulder. "Don't run off again."

She tried to push him away but something wasn't right, she couldn't properly draw a breath and her chest suddenly felt tight. Dale tried to keep hold of her but she finally broke his grip. Stepping back, hands on her knees, she noticed the doorman had gone.

STORMBLADE PRODUCTIONS

"How did you find me?"

"It was the Devil's own job," he said and nodded at someone behind her. "I had to have a friend help."

Polly whirled around to see a smiling Mr Creepy in the middle of the street.

"I see you," he said and she screamed, turning on her heel and pushing past Dale. The end of the street seemed so far away, the fog colouring everything grey so she could only discern people and cars as darker smudges.

Running hurt. Her throat felt blocked, as if she'd swallowed something and it was lodged there. She tried to cough but that didn't shift it. Her head began to throb and she could hear a high-pitched whistle that might have been behind her, might have been in her head.

She touched her throat and flashes of light spread across her line of vision, like a hundred tiny fireworks disappearing as soon as they'd burned.

It was getting harder to breathe.

The throbbing increased, along with the whistle.

Her head felt heavy, her arms cumbersome.

She reached for the wall, trying to keep on her feet, but when she staggered, she realised the wall wasn't there at all.

Realised nothing was there.

Only darkness, punctuated by those peculiar flashes.

She opened her eyes.

STORMBLADE PRODUCTIONS

Eleven

Manu's face filled her vision, snarling as he pressed his thumbs into her windpipe. She grabbed for his hands, tried to pull his thumbs away as stars burst, pure and white, above his head.

"La putain," he hissed.

Polly couldn't breathe and heard the high whistling sound again as he leaned forward, his mouth inches from her own. She dug her nails into the back of his hands and felt his flesh give. He gritted his teeth, hissing the pain between them so she pressed harder until he relaxed his grip. He back-handed her across the face as he pushed himself off the bed.

"Pute," he said, shaking his hand, "you fucking bitch."

She couldn't move, except to put her hands protectively to her throat. She watched him pace to the window and back like a caged animal.

"It should have been so easy, stupid gullible *rosbif pute*."

"Why?" Polly managed to say, the word dragged harshly against her throat.

He made a dismissive gesture and stalked to the window again. She pulled the duvet partly over herself.

"Pick up the stupid stray tourists," he said, and did his trousers up, pulling the belt tight. "Show them a good time, get them drunk and then take what you want." He found his shirt and put it on, standing in front of the window as he buttoned it up. "But you? Oh no, you didn't fucking drink enough, did you?"

Polly bit her lip to stem the flow of tears. She didn't understand any of this, was completely disorientated, but knew she had to hold it together. "What?"

"This!" he yelled, holding his arms out and turning in a complete circle. "You didn't pass out." He shook his head, disgusted. "Fucking pute."

She tried to sit up but he snarled and took a step towards her. "Stay on your back, I need to think."

Polly struggled to try and piece together what had happened. The club, the little café, everything going so well, back here and that experience and now this. What was she missing?

Manu ran a hand through his hair. "Stupide," he said, looking at the floor, "stupide."

STORMBLADE PRODUCTIONS

A single sob escaped and she put a hand over her mouth to stifle any more. He glanced at her, his hair falling into his eyes. "Get up," he said.

She looked at him, waiting for him to say something else, unsure if she'd misheard or misunderstood.

"Get up," he said, his voice rising.

Polly sat on the edge of the bed and pulled the duvet around her.

"Up!"

She stood, her legs unsteady. "Please," she said, trying to keep her voice level, "don't hurt me."

"Turn around and go into the bathroom," he said and took a step towards her.

Polly yelped and took a step back. "I can't turn my back on you."

"Turn around Polly."

"I…" She couldn't turn because she was too scared of what he might do. He reached out and she flinched but he only put his hand on her right shoulder.

"You need to turn around," he said, slowly and calmly.

"Manu…"

He slid his hand along her collarbone quickly, gripped the base of her throat and pushed. She was closer to the wall than she'd realised and only knew when her head bounced off it. The flashes came back only to slowly absorb into a dark curtain that eventually obscured Manu too.

Cold stone woke her and pain rushed into the back of her head, making her groan. She was in shadow, her eyes unfocussed, looking at a haze of shimmering flowers of light. She tried to move but a wave of nausea made her stop and she took a deep breath, blinking a few times to clear the tears.

Manu was kneeling down a few feet away on a cobbled path, his back to her. She felt fear come rushing back like a train, pulling her chest tight and making it hard to breathe. She lay still, trying to calm herself and regulate her breathing. Adrenalin was pumping through her; she was more scared than she'd ever been but she was also alive and the only way to stay like that was to calm down.

Polly took another deep breath, let it out slowly. It wasn't brilliant, but it was better - if she got out of this in one piece, then she could fall apart. Carefully, gently, she glanced around and seemed to be lying on cobblestones between a thick tree and an ornate metalwork bench. Behind her a steep stone wall rose up high, more bright lights beyond it. Ahead, Manu was looking over the lip of something. Was it a path? She looked beyond him, squinting at the light. Was that the cathedral?

She patted herself down; nothing seemed to be broken and she realised she was wearing her dress again, which he must have put on.

Manu got to his feet, muttering under his breath. A car with a rumbling exhaust drove by above her and it suddenly clicked where she was. She'd seen it before but couldn't remember when - it felt like ages ago. Was it on her walking tour this morning or in a book? The footpath that ran along the Seine.

Another thought swam to the surface - the Necktie Murderer.

But no, that was rubbish. Manu had talked about taking what he wanted and he didn't mean sex, he meant something more like money or jewellery.

STORMBLADE PRODUCTIONS

He walked over, his shoes crunching loose bits of grit, and she squinted her eyes, not wanting to close them completely because she had to see what was going on. He knelt in front of her face and she was glad to be in shadow.

"Putain de pute!" he muttered, repeating the phrase again and again, clearly scared. He pinched her cheeks between thumb and forefinger, forcing her mouth open, and leaned in close enough that she could feel his breath. "Why? Putain!"

He squeezed harder and she couldn't hold back the anguished cry. Getting to his feet, he grabbed her shoulders and roughly pulled her out of the shadow towards the bench.

"Niquer!" he shouted and pushed her down, "why won't you stay knocked out?"

Polly scrabbled back until she hit the wall and pushed herself up into a squat, looking left and right. The walkway was deserted but bright lamps lit everything except the area closest to the wall. Stone steps led upwards at intervals and she was midway between two sets.

"Why make life so fucking difficult for me?"

Polly could sense the fear clouding her mind again and shook it away. "You're a thief," she said, her throat still tight.

A manic expression crossed his face. "What did you expect?"

What had she been expecting? A nice man, maybe, having a blow-out after a hard day in the city, trawling little nightclubs to find a one-night stand? "Not a thief," she said finally.

STORMBLADE PRODUCTIONS

He barked out a little laugh. "And I didn't expect you to be like this, but now what do I do, you know who I am."

She felt the tingle of adrenalin in her fingertips. "Let me go, we both walk away."

He laughed again. "I can't trust you," he said, looking sad. He shook his head and loosened his tie. "Non, ma cherie. This has to finish now."

"It doesn't," she implored him, "it really doesn't."

He walked towards her, fiddling with his tie. He hadn't undone it and was adjusting the knot so he could tighten the loop. It only took her a moment to realise what he was doing.

"I am sorry, ma cherie, but this must be the way. I cannot allow you to tell."

"Don't do this," she said, wishing she hadn't backed up to the wall. He was five paces away, but with the bench to her left and the tree to her right, there wasn't enough space to go either way. The adrenalin was now coursing through her as he advanced, adjusting the knot.

Could she push him out of the way? If she sprang at him, would he react quickly enough or could she knock him over and run for the stairs? Another car drove by above her head and that made up her mind.

"Help me!" she screamed, "aidez-moi, aidez-moi!"

He rushed at her and she screamed again, wordlessly this time. His hand clamped over her mouth and he pulled her down to the left, rolling so she landed on top of him. He let go of her face, held her waist and twisted his body to the left so she rolled off him. He was up in an instant, sitting on her chest, his knees braced against her arms, her hands trapped.

STORMBLADE PRODUCTIONS

Polly screamed as he grabbed a handful of hair, pulling her head up from the cobbles. He slipped the tie over and pulled the knot, cutting off her scream as her throat constricted. She heard the whistling again and tried to suck in air that wasn't there, a band of white light playing at the edge of her vision. She tried to lift her head but it was difficult to move. A line of spittle ran off his lips and onto her nose, and her eyelids flickered. The whistling was loud now and, just below it, she could hear a fading beat.

He was killing her.

With the last of her strength, she tried to move her hands, buried as they were between her stomach and his - what? She couldn't tell, her brain slowly fogging over. She made as much of a claw with her fingers as she could and pressed upwards. There was resistance at first and then he howled in pain and pushed back, his knees leaving her arms.

She managed to free her hands and push him back. He didn't topple but he let go of the tie long enough for her to get her fingers under the loop. He struggled to get back on her chest but she bucked her hips and got more fingers under the loop so when he tried to pull it she was ready for him.

He squatted over her and Polly brought her left leg up quickly, her knee clouting his groin. His breath woofed out in a wounded cry and he fell to the side, letting go of the tie. She pulled it loose and rolled away, gasping for breath, trying to fill her lungs. She got to her hands and knees, her head on the cobbles as another wave of nausea crashed over her. When it passed she looked up.

Manu was on his hands and knees, coming towards her.

Polly got to her feet unsteadily and looked behind her. The edge of the walkway was three, maybe four paces away, the dark water of the Seine barely visible. All she could hear, above her ragged breathing, was the sound of it slapping against the stones.

"Pute!" Manu said, getting closer.

"Keep back," she said, desperate now.

"Too late," he said and pushed forward, getting to his feet as he moved so he connected with her upper thighs in a tackle. Polly tried to stay up but he had weight and momentum on his side and pulled her down sideways. She twisted as she fell and landed on him, his face between her side and the cobbles. She slid off and he rolled with her, getting on top though the fall had hurt him. A smear of blood swept across his mouth and cheeks and his nose was clearly broken. He pressed his thumbs into her throat but she got her hands over his, digging her nails in until he cried out. She kneed him again, catching the back of his thigh. Enough to unseat him, he fell to her left and his forehead cracked against the cobbles.

He didn't move.

Polly looked up at the stars, hands across her throat, then at him.

She got unsteadily to her feet, her head spinning with dizziness, and she bent forward, hands on her knees, until it passed. Manu still hadn't moved. She kicked him hard in the ribs and backed away, not taking her eyes from him until she was at the staircase. He hadn't moved but she daren't risk it, so backed up the stairs slowly, holding the wall for support, her heels scuffing each riser.

By the time she reached the street, she was exhausted, but Manu hadn't moved and she was free. The hands

STORMBLADE PRODUCTIONS

grabbing her arm made her shriek and she turned, not knowing what to expect.

"Pol!"

She looked at Dale, not quite believing it was him. He stared at her, looking both startled and frightened. "Pol?" he said again, "what the hell happened?"

She looked down. Her forearms were covered in bruises, there was blood on her fingertips and one of the straps had broken on her dress. Her bare feet were grubby.

She didn't want to answer him, didn't want him to know. "How did you find me?"

"I was worried about you, love," he said, his expression softening. "After I checked the credit card, I downloaded that app that lets you track mobiles."

"You tracked me?"

"I love you, I needed to know…"

STORMBLADE PRODUCTIONS

Over his shoulder she could see a tall broad man wearing a rugby shirt and jeans running towards them. Behind him, a woman was digging into her handbag.

"So you followed me?"

The man was getting closer. Polly tried to shake Dale's hand off but he held her tighter.

"I had to, Polly, don't you see? We have too much history to throw it away."

"You're a bastard," she said, and then the man was right behind them. He put his arm around Dale's throat and pulled him away. Dale staggered a couple of steps, bounced off the wall and slid down to sit on the pavement. The man stood over him, fists against his sides, while the woman ran to Polly, holding a mobile phone in her hand. Dale looked from Polly to the man and back again.

STORMBLADE PRODUCTIONS

"Who the hell are you?" asked Dale indignantly. The man said something Polly didn't catch. "I can't speak French," said Dale, "but this is my wife, I didn't do this to her."

"J'appelle la police," the woman said, and Polly watched as she took in the bruises, blood and ripped strap.

"Oui, merci," said Polly.

"What was that?" asked Dale, "what did she say?"

Ignoring him, the woman touched Polly's arm gently. "Que s'est-il passé?" she asked - what happened?

Polly glanced at Dale who looked pathetic, pressed against the wall, his eyes big and scared. She looked at the woman and took a deep breath. "He gets like this sometimes," she said in halting French, not wanting to get it wrong.

Nodding, the woman called across to her partner, repeating Polly's words, and he growled, bunching his fists tighter. The woman put the phone to her ear and spoke rapidly.

The police car dropped Polly outside L'Hotel Truffaut at eleven o'clock and she waved as it drove away.

She felt dazed and lost.

Polly told the police about Manu as soon as they arrived, but didn't correct what she'd said to the lovely woman - who was called Gilberte Doinel and gave Polly her anorak to keep her warm - and so Dale was taken in for questioning too. She'd heard nothing of him since. Manu, she was told, was badly injured and had been taken to hospital under police guard.

After being checked over, she'd spent most of the night and early morning with L'inspecteur Cabanel and told him everything, from finding Dale in her house to what happened in the hotel room. L'inspecteur didn't say a great deal but he seemed aware of the scam Manu was carrying out. After a second, much briefer interview with a woman who wore thick glasses and a very tight bun, Polly was allowed to go on condition she didn't leave the country for a couple of days. She agreed. On her way out, one of the policewomen who'd sat in on the interview found her an old pair of trainers to replace the slippers she'd been offered when she first arrived.

The sun was warm on her face and she smiled, happy to be alive. She didn't want to go back to the hotel yet, didn't feel like she could face it, and walked to the brasserie instead. The tables had been set up outside and several were occupied, people drinking coffee and beer as they watched the world go by. Polly looked at the cathedral and decided she'd visit it today.

She noticed someone sitting alone at a table, wearing a baseball cap and dark glasses. Closer still, Polly realised it was Katrina and sat opposite her.

Katrina didn't move. "Sorry," she said, "I'm waiting for someone."

"I know," said Polly.

Katrina looked up, shielding her face from the sun with her hand. "Hey."

"You look like death, did you have a good night?"

"No, we stayed on drinking for a while after you went, then he took me back to my hotel, showed me a good time and when I woke up this morning, the bastard had cleared me out."

"Bugger."

"Yup, I know, right?" She took a sip of coffee then looked at Polly again. "Hey, are you alright?"

"Not really."

Katrina took off her glasses gingerly. "Jesus, what the hell happened to you?"

"It's a long story," said Polly. "Shall I get us both a coffee?"

Afterword

"Polly" was one of those enjoyable writing experiences where everything seemed to come together at once as each disparate part of the puzzle slotted nicely in with its neighbour. As most writers will tell you, it doesn't happen like that very often.

This all started with a Facebook message in August 2015 from Neil Buchanan at Stormblade Productions (I reviewed his "Everett Smiles" audio book, which his sister Carrie narrated), asking if I'd like to write something for him. As I'd never had an audio book of my work done before, I readily agreed, though I had no idea what I was going to write. As it was, the main element came to me as

STORMBLADE PRODUCTIONS

I was driving with my family to Northampton in late August - we were listening to INXS and "New Sensation" came on and the title struck me. Since Carrie was going to narrate, I'd already decided I was going to have a female protagonist (why have a terrific female voice actor and not take advantage of that?) and so a new sensation could be a bloke or a destination... the first blocks fell into place.

Since horror is my default genre, that was my original intent (at first, Polly wasn't going to make it to the end) but the tone gradually shifted as I worked on the notes. I had most of the story in my head by the time FantasyCon came round in late October, where I met Carrie in person for the first time and we got on brilliantly. I pitched the idea to her and Vix Kirkpatrick late on the Saturday night as we chatted with Pete May in the bar and they loved it. On the Sunday, Carrie sought me out to pitch it to Neil - she

STORMBLADE PRODUCTIONS

remembered loving it but couldn't explain it to him - and he liked it, so I was off.

I started writing in November but was still having trouble with the ending - I wrote my original idea out, which saw Polly walk away from her encounter with Manu, thinking back to how she'd killed Dale and Freya. I met up with my friend Sue Moorcroft at The Trading Post and we talked the sequence through and she helped me formulate the idea of what happened in the story you just read.

The first draft was written over the course of a month, I took a fortnight off before spending a week writing the second draft and sent that to my band of pre-readers. Using their feedback and my own thoughts, I revised it again in January and sent it to Neil who accepted it. Thankfully.

STORMBLADE PRODUCTIONS

The location for the bulk of the story, the Latin Quarter of Paris, saw me utilising that old adage of 'write what you know'. Like Polly, I'd wanted to visit the Left Bank since my teens and finally got my chance ten years ago when I began working for an American company who decided to have us, the UK branch, look after the French office. Luckily, the manager (a fine chap called Emmanuel, who everyone called Manu) was very friendly and loved his city so after the working day was done, he showed us around, took us to places we wanted to see and fed us in fine restaurants. On one such visit, I said I'd like to see Notre Dame but the road was clogged with traffic so I got out and walked alongside the Seine to the great Cathedral and waited for them to catch up. I took lots of pictures and enjoyed the sensation of wandering in the Latin Quarter,

STORMBLADE PRODUCTIONS

listening to the people and music around me and realised the Left Bank was everything I had always hoped it would be.

A few years later, a colleague & I went to Paris for a meeting which we managed to wrap up by lunchtime. After a very nice meal, we said goodbye to our hosts, took the metro to Notre Dame and had a drink in the brasserie (the Hotel Notre Dame St Michel, which is the same one Polly uses) on the corner as we decided what to do. Since it was a gloriously sunny May afternoon, we walked alongside the river to the Louvre, taking in the Bouquinistes and the Love-Locks on the Pont Des Artes bridge and had a lovely time. It's the same walk Polly does (though ours didn't get as far as the park) and when it came time to re-create it, I used Google maps extensively and it felt like I was back there.

Most of my work features some form of in-joke and "Polly" is no exception. I'm not sure where her name came from (though in my head she looks like Carrie and carries herself like my best friend Pauline), or Dale's, but Katrina is based on a friend and colleague (called Katrina) I met when I was at our Head Office in Detroit. For the rest, I decided to tap into one of my favourite film - "The 400 Blows" - which is not only a wonderful piece of cinema, it's also set in Paris. Polly stays in L'Hotel Truffaut (named for Francois, the director) and all the names come from either the actors or the characters in the film. The one exception is the disco where Polly meets Manu – another favourite film of mine is "Pauline a la Plage", directed by Eric Rohmer, so he lent his name to

STORMBLADE PRODUCTIONS

Club Eric. Most people won't notice (or care) of course but I'd like to think a fan might read the novella and make the connection.

In real life, Paris was everything I wanted it to be and more - a working city, certainly and as beautiful and grimy as London can be - but the architecture, the atmosphere and the sense of all who've gone before is just wonderful. I hope I managed to capture at least some of that here.

Au revoir!

Mark West

STORMBLADE PRODUCTIONS

Mark West was born in Northamptonshire in 1969 and now lives there with his wife Alison and their young son Matthew. Since discovering the small press in 1998 he has published over eighty short stories, two novels (*In The Rain With The Dead* and *Conjure*), a novelette (*The Mill*), a chapbook (*What Gets Left Behind*), a collection (*Strange Tales*) and two novellas (*Drive,* which was nominated for a British Fantasy Award and *The Lost Film*). He has more short stories and novellas forthcoming and is currently working on a novel.

Away from writing, he enjoys reading, walking, cycling, watching films and playing Dudeball with his son.

STORMBLADE PRODUCTIONS

He can be contacted through his website at

www.markwest.org.uk and is also on Twitter as

@MarkEWest

STORMBLADE PRODUCTIONS